OXFORD
UNIVERSITY PRESS

Great Clarendon Street, Oxford OX2 6DP

Oxford University Press is a department of the University of Oxford.
It furthers the University's objective of excellence in research, scholarship,
and education by publishing worldwide in

Oxford   New York

Auckland Cape Town Dar es Salaam Hong Kong Karachi
Kuala Lumpur Madrid Melbourne Mexico City Nairobi
New Delhi Shanghai Taipei Toronto

With offices in

Argentina Austria Brazil Chile Czech Republic France Greece
Guatemala Hungary Italy Japan Poland Portugal Singapore
South Korea Switzerland Thailand Turkey Ukraine Vietnam
Oxford is a registered trade mark of Oxford University Press
in the UK and in certain other countries

British Library Cataloguing in Publication Data

Data available

ISBN-13: 978-0-19-278235-9 (Hardback)
ISBN-10: 0-19-278235-5 (Hardback)
ISBN-13: 978-0-19-272393-2 (Paperback)
ISBN-10: 0-19-272393-6 (Paperback)
ISBN-13: 978-0-19-275479-0 (Paperback with audio CD)
ISBN-10: 0-19-275479-3 (Paperback with audio CD)

1 3 5 7 9 10 8 6 4 2

Printed in China by Imago

The Elves
and the
Shoemaker

Ian Beck

OXFORD
UNIVERSITY PRESS

Once upon a time, when the world was young and snow fell every winter, there lived a shoemaker and his wife. He was a fine craftsman, but recently trade had not been good, and they were very poor. The time came when the shoemaker had only one piece of leather left – enough to make just one pair of shoes. So, that evening, he sat in his cold workshop and cut out the leather into all the shapes he needed for the shoes.

Then his wife called him in for their supper, and so he wearily left all the cut-out pieces on the bench ready to make up in the morning.

After a poor supper of watery cabbage soup and scraps, the shoemaker and his wife lit their last candle and made their way to bed.

When the shoemaker opened his workshop door in the morning he had the shock of his life. There on the bench stood the finest pair of shoes he had ever seen. He looked around for the pieces of leather but everything was tidy as always. Then he called to his wife to come, and together they peered closely at the shoes. It was his leather all right but the stitches were tiny and neat.

'Made by a master hand, much finer than my own,' he said. 'But where did they come from?'

'No matter,' said his wife. 'Let us be glad. These shoes will make our fortune, you'll see.' And she put the shoes in the middle of the shop window.

It was not long before the shoes were noticed. A gentleman came in and tried them on. Walking up and down the shop, he said they were the most comfortable and handsome shoes he had ever worn, and he happily paid twice the normal price for them.

Now there was enough money to buy leather to make two pairs of shoes, and even some left over for a good supper.

That evening the shoemaker cut out the leather and left the pieces ready for making up in the morning; and that night the soup was thicker and tastier, and the shoemaker and his wife went to bed well satisfied.

And sure enough, in the morning, when the shoemaker opened his workshop, there were two pairs of perfectly made shoes, all complete with their tiny stitching, and the leather soft and glossy with polish.

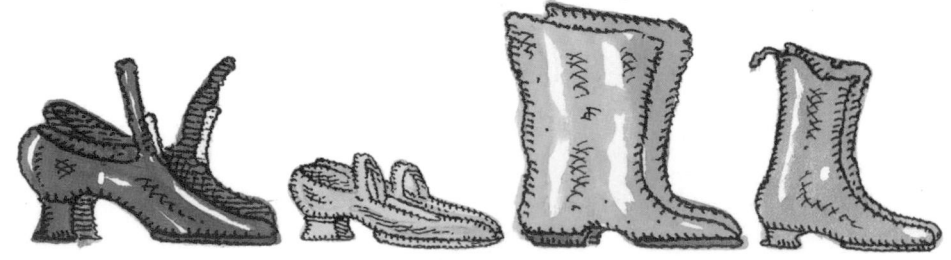

The shoes were soon sold, and the shoemaker was able to buy enough leather to make four pairs of shoes. Again the shoemaker carefully cut out the patterns, and again in the morning there stood four more pairs of exquisite shoes, and so it went on.

The shoemaker was able to buy more and more leather in all the colours of the rainbow.

He cut out pieces for a great variety of shoes, and pumps, and slippers, and boots. Every morning he would come in to find them all perfectly finished as before.

He was soon thought to be the best shoemaker in the land, and one morning the king himself arrived with his page and chancellor and bought an especially fine pair of high boots in green leather.

One night the shoemaker and his wife decided to hide themselves in the workshop to see who it was at work. They left a tall candle on the workbench, and then settled in their hiding place to wait.

When the clock chimed midnight a pair of strange little figures climbed up on to the workbench. They were tiny, not much bigger than a shoe themselves, and they wore very

odd clothes: acorn halves for hats, leaves and grasses and scraps for clothes. 'Elves,' gasped the shoemaker.

The elves worked hard and fast. They stitched with tiny needles, and hammered with tiny hammers, and buffed and polished with little cloths.

They worked all through the night and didn't stop until the candle was almost burnt down and daylight showed through the frosty window. Then the two elves scuttled back under the door, leaving a line of beautiful shoes on the bench.

The shoemaker and his wife crept out of their hiding place.

'Did you ever see anything like it?' said the shoemaker. 'Those elves have helped us to make our fortune. And did you see what they were wearing? Just little scraps, and acorns, and bits and bobs. They must be frozen in this weather.' And the shoemaker and his wife shook their heads.

'I have an idea,' said the shoemaker's wife. 'We shall make some fine clothes for them, as a way of saying thank you.'

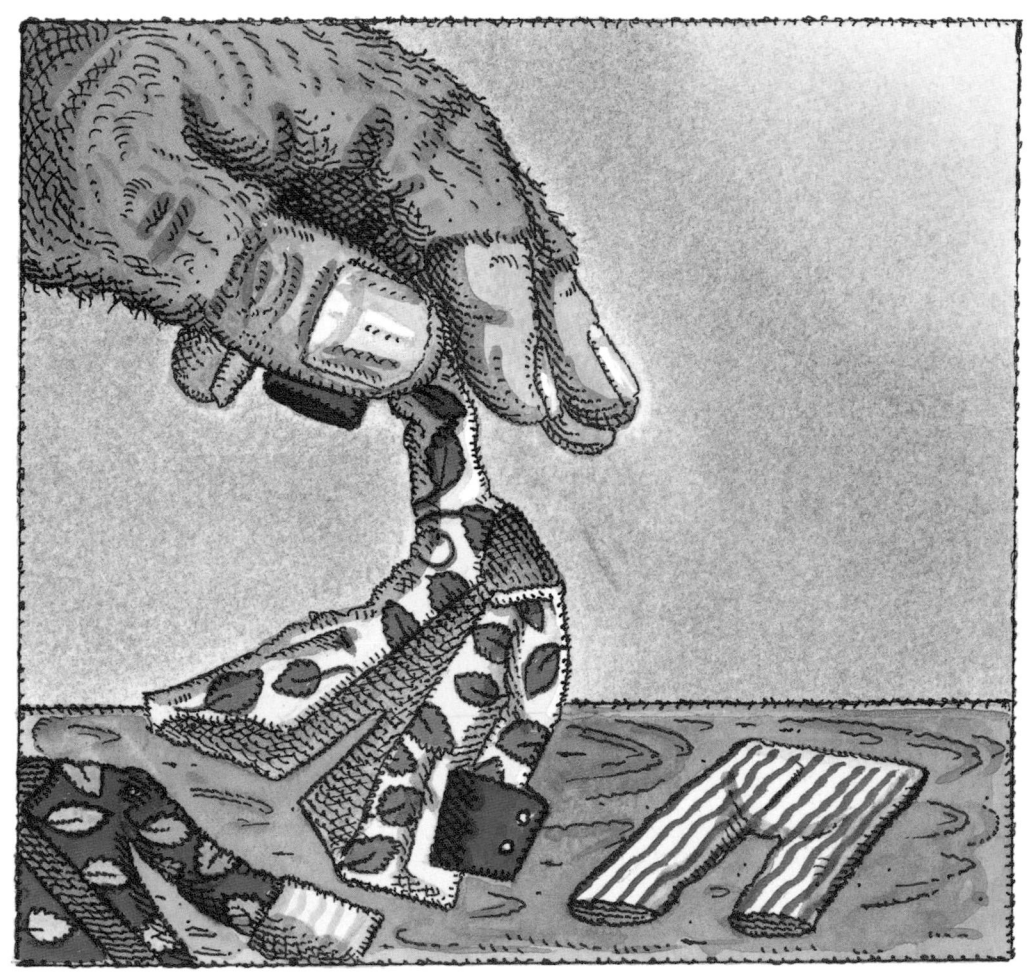

So, during the day (which was Christmas Eve), the shoemaker and his wife cut and sewed with their nimble fingers.

They made some little shirts, and waistcoats, and jackets, and breeches, and even stockings and mittens. They used pieces of brocade, velvet, silk, cambric, and fine wool.

That night they laid out all the little clothes on the workbench, and again settled themselves in their hiding place to wait.

Sure enough, as the clock chimed midnight the two elves appeared. They climbed up to the workbench, where they found all the fine

new clothes, beautifully cut and sewn. The elves put on their new clothes, laughing and chattering to themselves.

'Happy Christmas, little men,' whispered the shoemaker and his wife.

Then the elves danced round the candlestick, and as they danced they sang,

'Now we're dressed so fine and neat
We'll no more work for others' feet.'

And then they danced off the bench, under the door, and were never seen again.

The shoemaker and his wife hung a smart new sign on the front of their shop; it was cut out in the shape of an elegant shoe, and there was a crown to show that even the king was one of their customers.

The shoemaker and his wife lived happily and prospered until the end of their days, which was a very long time indeed.